For Hannah,
all-by-herself
M.W.

For Georgie
and Eddie Huntley
P.B.

First published by Candlewick Press

CANDLEWICK PRESS
2067 MASSACHUSETTS AVENUE
CAMBRIDGE MA 02140

ISBN 0-590-58284-4

Text copyright © 1975 by Martin Waddell.
Illustrations copyright © 1992 by Patrick Benson. All rights reserved. Published by Scholastic Inc., 555 Broadway, New York, NY 10012, by arrangement with Candlewick Press.

12 11 10 9 8 7 6 5 4 3 2 1   5 6 7 8 9/9 0/0

Printed in the U.S.A.   08

First Scholastic printing, October 1995

OWL BABIES

Written by
Martin Waddell

Illustrated by
Patrick Benson

CANDLEWICK PRESS
CAMBRIDGE, MASSACHUSETTS

Once there were three baby owls:
Sarah and Percy and Bill.
They lived in a hole
in the trunk of a tree
with their Owl Mother.
The hole had twigs and
leaves and owl feathers in it.
It was their house.

One night they woke up and
their Owl Mother was GONE.
"Where's Mommy?" asked Sarah.
"Oh my goodness!" said Percy.
"I want my mommy!" said Bill.

The baby owls *thought*
(all owls think a lot) –
"I think she's gone hunting," said Sarah.
"To get us our food!" said Percy.
"I want my mommy!" said Bill.

But their Owl Mother didn't come.
The baby owls came out of
their house, and they sat
on the tree and waited.

A big branch for Sarah,
a small branch for Percy,
and an old piece of ivy for Bill.
"She'll be back," said Sarah.
"Back *soon*!" said Percy.
"I want my mommy!" said Bill.

It was dark in the woods and
they had to be brave, for things
moved all around them.
"She'll bring us mice and
things that are nice," said Sarah.
"I suppose so!" said Percy.
"I want my mommy!" said Bill.

They sat and they thought
(all owls think a lot) –
"I think we should *all*

sit on *my* branch," said Sarah.
And they did,
all three together.

"Suppose she got lost," said Sarah.

"Or a fox got her!" said Percy.

"I want my mommy!" said Bill.

And the baby owls closed
their owl eyes and wished their
Owl Mother would come.

AND SHE CAME.

Soft and silent, she swooped
through the trees
to Sarah and Percy
and Bill.

"Mommy!" they cried,
and they flapped and they danced,
and they bounced up and down
on their branch.

"WHAT'S ALL THE FUSS?"
their Owl Mother asked.
"You knew I'd come back."
The baby owls thought
(all owls think a lot) –
"I knew it," said Sarah.
"And I knew it!" said Percy.
"I love my mommy!" said Bill.